PAPA AND THE LITTLE QUEEN

A WALK WITH ST. THERESE

BY

KATHLEEN VINCENZ

DEDICATION

To St. Thérèse for showing us a simpler way to love,
and to Danny for living in that spirit.

CONTENTS

A WALK

Thérèse held her gray schoolbook close to her face until it bumped her nose.

She wrinkled her forehead.

She squinted her eyes.

She concentrated.

What was that word? Her eyes followed the high peaks of its first letter to the low valleys of its next.

"H … H-e … H-e-a."

Her brain lit up. "Heaven! The word was Heaven!"

A heavenly word to read. And a heavenly word to tell Papa.

Thérèse rushed down the wooden steps of her house and out to the garden where she knew Papa would be resting. She skipped past her altars tucked into the crevices of the stone wall that encircled the garden.

In the altar to Mary, the dainty bluebells sang her praises.

In the altar to the child Jesus, the happy yellow daises cheered.

And in the altar to the Lord, the sweetness of the prim red rose floated to Heaven.

Heaven. H-E-A-V-E-N. She could read that word! She must tell Papa!

Near her altars, she kept the make-believe tea she made from seeds and bark.

"I'll serve Papa my tea."

She poured the tea into her doll's teacup, and it trickled gold and shimmery, like real jasmine. She inhaled the earth and sunshine that rose from it.

Thérèse crept close to Papa who sat straight in his chair in the center of the garden. Papa rubbed his beard in thought and stared into the heavens. She tapped his knee.

"Papa! I'm here! Surprise!"

Papa shifted his shining eyes to Thérèse and smiled. "Ah, I was saying to God Almighty how thirsty I was, and how I needed a *petite reine*, a little queen, to bring me tea."

"Oh, Papa. God told me, and I'm here." Thérèse handed him the teacup, and Papa pressed it to his lips. Thérèse knew he didn't drink it, but she didn't mind. She didn't drink it either!

"I have a better surprise, Papa. Today I read my first word." Thérèse breathed in her sadness. "It's where Mama is. Can you guess what word I read, Papa?"

"Hmmm …"

Papa wrinkled his forehead.

He scratched his head.

He studied the air.

He concentrated.

Thérèse rubbed away Papa's frown lines. "I will tell you. It's Heaven. The word I learned to read is Heaven. I know that if I'm ever bad, I'll fly to Heaven where Mama is and she will hold me tight, and I'll be safe."

"Shall we celebrate, my little queen?" Papa swung her high up onto his shoulders with his laughing sad face near hers.

"Oh, Papa." Thérèse clapped. "Yes! Where should we go? What should we do?"

"First, we visit the Lord."

"To the Lord." Thérèse laughed and pointed toward town.

...

Once outside their garden wall, Papa's feet crunched along a gravel road that led into the busy center of the town of Lisieux and their church, the Cathedral of St. Peter.

After a bit more crunching of Papa's feet along the gravel, Papa turned onto a brick road that led them between tall brick and wooden homes and buildings already hundreds of years old, with crisscrossing wooden decorations and ground floors that were smaller than the higher floors.

"I'm waving to Uncle!" Thérèse announced as they passed a pharmacy shop where Uncle made medicines. Thérèse knew that Papa had moved the family to Lisieux after Mama died to be near relatives, like Uncle, who lived in Lisieux and could help them. She waved more at the thought of his kindness.

Further on, they passed a gray building with a pitched roof and a small cross perched on top.

"Look, little queen, the Chapel of the Carmel," Papa said as they neared. "Behind that grating are holy nuns who spend their days in prayer to God Almighty."

"Will I be one, Papa?" Thérèse placed her hands together like the steeples of a church.

"Only God Almighty knows."

Thérèse wondered when God Almighty would let her know if she would be a nun. Somehow, deep in her heart, she knew the Chapel of the Carmel would make a lovely home for her. But not yet. She patted Papa's head. Now she'd stay with Papa.

As they entered the busy section of town, Papa and Thérèse walked past busy, bustling people buying fish so they would be ready for Friday when they could eat no meat.

Among the busy shoppers, a man dragged himself along with wooden crutches in the opposite direction. Thérèse's heart squeezed at the sight of him.

"Let me down, Papa."

She slid down and dug deep into her pocket. She held out a penny for the man. "For you!"

The man with his hard, brown face and tattered and dirty clothes, studied the penny and then Thérèse. Thérèse wondered why he didn't take the penny. Was he deciding how to spend it, maybe for food or new clothes, or for a wash in the public bath. Which would she do?

Suddenly, smile wrinkles erupted around the man's eyes and he smiled at Thérèse. He shook his head.

"No," he said. "Not a penny, but I'll take the sunbeam that shone in my life today, from you, little one."

"Ah, she is my queen." Papa wrapped his hand warm around Thérèse's, and they went ahead to the church.

"**S**hh now, little queen," Papa warned as they entered.

The holy water at the entrance cooled Thérèse's skin as she dipped her fingers into the bowl for a blessing. She pressed:

Fingertips to forehead.

Fingertips to shoulders.

Fingertips to heart!

Papa and Thérèse walked down the narrow aisle that led to the altar, lined with angel statues whose wings swooped upward to Heaven. At their pew near the front, Papa and Thérèse knelt. They bowed in prayer.

Thérèse peeked. "Oh, Papa, look! They are putting Jesus in the sacred vessel." Thérèse's head nodded on the word *Jesus*.

"They put Him in the monstrance," Papa agreed.

Indeed, the priest at the altar had placed the Host of Jesus in a sacred vessel with its glory shooting out in beams. Before touching the vessel, the priest had wrapped his hands in his gold-embroidered purple robes so that he didn't touch it.

Then, the priest lifted the vessel of Jesus over his head toward Heaven and walked down the aisle passing Thérèse and Papa and out the church door and into the street.

"He's taking the Lord out for a celebration! A celebration of Jesus. Let's celebrate too!" Thérèse tugged at Papa's hand in happiness to follow.

The others in the church stood and crowded out of the church with Thérèse and Papa.

Outside, Thérèse dropped Papa's hand and skipped along beside the sacred vessel held high. Her heart danced as she now skipped through the same streets of Lisieux that they'd just walked.

A woman standing outside her house handed Thérèse a rose from her garden.

"For you," the woman said, touching Thérèse's cheek.

"For the Lord!" Thérèse plucked the petals of the rose and tossed them up. Up with all her love for Jesus. The petals filled the air and flitted down, down around the sacred vessel like a shower of roses from Heaven.

Thérèse lifted her arms for Papa to carry her as the crowd scurried on their way, and the priest returned Jesus to his safe home in the tabernacle of the church. "God can do anything, can't he, Papa? Even stay in a little host."

"Yes!" Papa swung her up. "Time for home, little queen."

"No, Papa, no! Fishing!"

Papa chuckled. "We have no fishing rods. How can we fish?"

…

As Thérèse knew he would, Papa didn't go home but followed the rocky path to his favorite stream, which ran clear and fast.

"See, Papa? See the bubbles?" Thérèse peered down to the bottom and pointed. "Those fish are laughing because we can't catch them. They are glad we have no fishing rods!"

Thérèse's heart beat happily too that they would not catch the fish. She carved a home for herself in the meadow next to the stream among its cornflowers, poppies, marguerites, and prickly, prickly grass!

The sound of a band drifted across the meadow from a faraway town. And then another sound. She laughed and parted the meadow grasses. *Snore!* The sound of Papa.

Thérèse sat still, as if she were back in church. Her heart melted soft and squishy, and floated up, up, to God Almighty in Heaven, Who came down, down, to Thérèse. God Almighty's greatness, His immenseness, loomed nearby.

Plop.

Plop. Plop.

Splash.

Splash. Splash.

Thérèse parted her meadow house and held up her palm to catch the drops. "Beautiful, jeweled drops are falling from Heaven."

Crash! Lightning flashed through the Heavens.

"The angels are shaking the sky too!" Thérèse lifted her face to catch the drops.

Papa awakened and ran toward her.

"My little queen, we must speed home, away from the lightning." Papa swooped her up.

"I don't want to leave, Papa. Joy, so much joy in Heaven. Look, Papa. I'm weeping more tears than the rain." Thérèse whisked a tear away with her finger.

"Yes, little queen, what a joyful day today was, but now for home."

Papa rushed with Thérèse safe in his arms down the brick roads to the gravel road, and up the path to their home, where the lights that gleamed in its many windows welcomed them.

As they walked to the door, the storm died, and the stars popped out to say goodnight.

"Look, Papa! Look! The angels wrote my letter in Heaven—a T." Thérèse pointed to the constellation Orion that appeared in the sky.

Shortly after, as Papa tucked her into bed, Thérèse asked, "Have I been good today? Is God pleased with me? Will Heaven and the Angels watch over me?"

"Yes, always yes, little queen. Heaven will always watch."

Heaven. She could read that word!

ABOUT THE LITTLE QUEEN

The Little Queen in the story is St. Thérèse, the beloved Catholic saint known as the Little Flower, who was born in 1873. She wrote about all the things she did with her Papa in her autobiography, *The Story of a Soul.*

Today if you walk through her town of Lisieux, France, you can still see her house with its many windows, called *Little Bushes,* and the church where she and Papa visited. The town is much different, however, than when she walked with her Papa.

The old homes with their crisscross decorations that Thérèse and Papa walked by are no longer there. Much of the town of Lisieux was destroyed during World War II. The next page shows a picture of some of the old homes of Lisieux.

The old homes of Lisieux

Also, a large church, called a *basilica*, looms over the town, built in honor of St. Thérèse and her simple ways of loving God. Hundreds of people fill the streets, especially during October, which is the month in which she is honored. It is her feast month.

Basilica St. Thérèse of Lisieux

And, God *did* know that Thérèse would become a nun and live her life in the convent Papa pointed to. She entered the convent when she was fifteen. All Thérèse's sisters became nuns too.

A nun is a woman who promises to live simply, pray often, and obey others. Because St. Thérèse lived in a house for nuns and never left it (called being *cloistered*), she shut herself away from the meadows and streams, unable to go fishing with Papa.

Also, being tucked away in the convent, she could only do little things to show her love of God and people. She couldn't lead an army, like St. Joan of Arc, argue with a Pope, like St. Teresa of Avila, or help the poor like Mother Therese.

Instead, she performed simple chores, like we all do:

Cleared the dinner dishes.

Scrubbed the floor.

Laundered the clothes in a wash pool.

She performed many good deeds, like helping a bad-tempered nun every night at dinner who complained about everything, and praying for missionaries in far-off lands where she would never visit.

For another sacrifice, she talked to other nuns during her breaks, instead of her sisters whom she loved very dearly. Breaks were important because it was the only time the nuns spoke. Along with vows of obedience and poverty, the nuns also took a vow of silence.

By doing all these things, St. Thérèse showed that loving in little ways was as important as loving in big ways— maybe even more difficult. She wrote about her Little Way in the same book she wrote about her walks with Papa, *The Story of a Soul*. She said:

> *The only way I can prove my love is by scattering flowers and these flowers are every little sacrifice, every glance and word, and the doing of the least actions for love.*

Thérèse's sister asked her to write *A Story of a Soul*. She wanted Thérèse to share the story of her life and how she had learned to love God.

Thérèse wrote her story in longhand on school paper on a writing box. In the story, she called herself a little flower of Jesus. Not a rose, or a lily, but a wildflower in a field, unnoticed but beautiful, like those she saw in the meadow that day with Papa, which is why she is called The Little Flower.

Even though she only did little things for God, she is a Doctor of the Catholic Church, meaning that her thoughts, writings, and actions show us in a special way how to be followers of Jesus.

Thérèse died of tuberculosis when she was twenty-four. After her death, her book caused a sensation. Copies of it sold out and they had to keep printing it. During World War I, soldiers carried pictures of Thérèse into battle. They called her "my little sister of the trenches."

We hope you will find her to be a little sister too, or even a little queen, to help you on your life journey.

PICTURES OF
PAPA AND THE LITTLE QUEEN

We often think of saints as living in the distant past when there were no cameras or televisions or the internet, so we can only imagine what they looked like unless someone painted their portrait.

However, St. Thérèse was born after the invention of the camera. Her sister Celine took her camera when she joined the convent, so we have many pictures of Thérèse, as well as what life was like inside the convent.

Here are a few.

Thérèse as a young girl

Thérèse's parents: her mother who died when Thérèse was four and her beloved Papa

St. Thérèse washing the laundry with her sister nuns

We, of course, at Squirrels at the Door Publishing are fond of the drawings of St. Thérèse by Danny Vincenz on our cover and the top of each chapter.

BIBLIOGRAPHY

Much of this story and dialogue come from St. Thérèse's writings, especially *The Story of a Soul*. I added a bit of dialogue of my own to help tell Thérèse's story.

Here are a few of my other resources:

Görres Ida Friederike. *The Hidden Face a Study of St Thérèse of Lisieux*. Ignatius Press, 2003.

Jeffreybruno. "Exclusive: St.Thérèse of Lisieux." *Aleteia*, 28 Dec. 2017, https://aleteia.org/2017/12/28/exclusive-st-therese-of-lisieux/.

Utilisateur, Super. "Aux Archives Du Carmel De Lisieux." *Site Des Archives Du Carmel De Lisieux*, https://www.archives-carmel-lisieux.fr/carmel/.

"Who Is St. Therese." *Society of the Little Flower*, 17 Aug. 2021, https://www.littleflower.org/st-therese/who-is-st-therese/.

ABOUT THE AUTHOR

Kathleen Vincenz is the author of *Papa and the Little Queen*, *Over the Falls in a Suitcase*, and *God's Sparrows*. She enjoys writing about family, faith, warmth, and humor. She lives on a hill with her husband and many woodland friends.

Find her books at Amazon and visit her website at squirrelsatthedoor.com to sign up for her newsletter with a bit of science, history, and reading and a lot of fun with a squirrel mascot, Larry.

Made in the USA
Middletown, DE
07 September 2023

38171058R00021